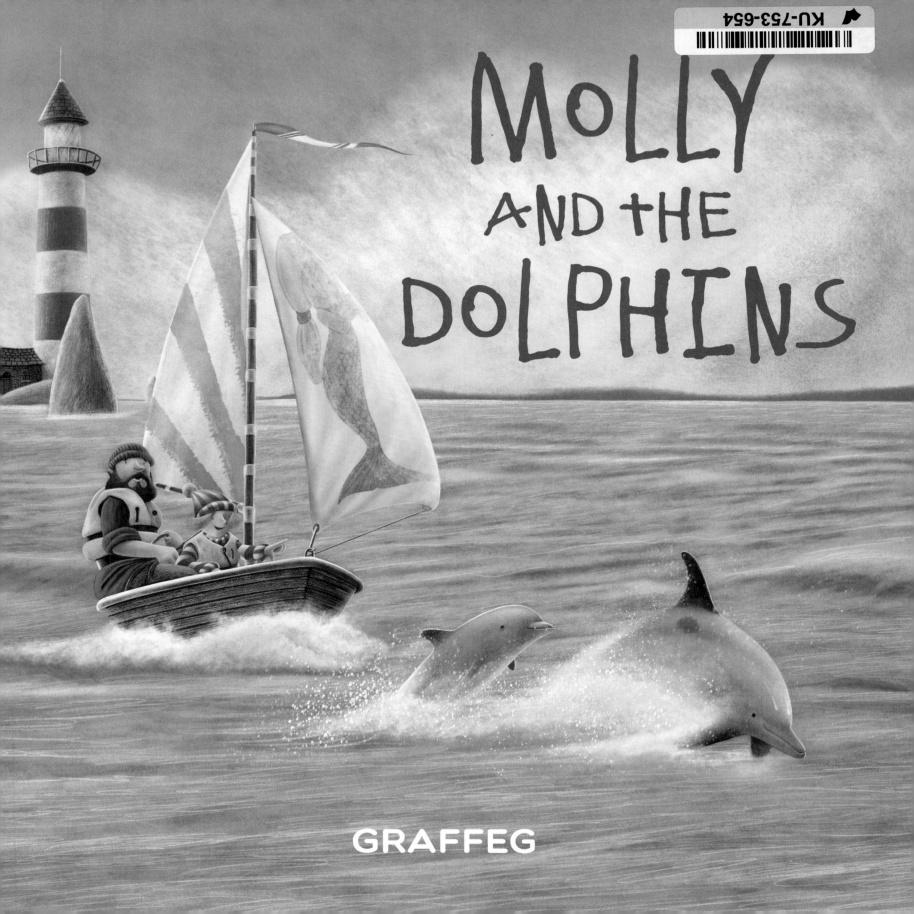

MOLLY
AND THE
DOLPHINS

GRAFFEG

'Molly,' said her father. 'I've a present for you.'

She followed him down to the harbour and there,
on the water, was a beautiful little boat.

'For me?' said Molly, amazed.

'I'll teach you to sail her,' said her father, smiling. 'I think you're old enough now.'

5

So every morning they went out in *The Mermaid*, as Molly called the lovely little dinghy he'd made for her.

Her father showed her how to read the wind, how to trim the sails and ride the waves.

'But you're not to try and sail her on your own,' he told her, firmly. 'Not till I know you're safe.'

6

'Look, Dad,' said Molly, one day. 'Dolphins!'

And there they were, all around *The Mermaid*, leaping and diving.

One of them, who Molly named Dot, became her special friend and swam with them every day.

And then there was a little mini-dolphin, swimming alongside.

'You've had a baby, Dot!' cried Molly. 'Well done, girl!'

At last Molly's father said she was ready to sail the boat by herself.

'I'll be close by, keeping an eye on you, but be careful,' he told her. 'The winds can whip up without warning.'

Molly sailed *The Mermaid* around the harbour and out past the lighthouse.

And it was so wonderful – just her and the sea!

Just Molly, the clouds and the sky and the sea!

Just her and the birds and her beautiful boat!

And then Molly spotted her friendly dolphin –
but there was something wrong. Very wrong.

Her baby was all tangled up in a fishing net.

'Oh you poor thing!' cried Molly. 'Dad! Dad!
Come and help!'

'Don't you fret,' said Molly's father to the young dolphin. 'I'll soon have you sorted.'

And with the mother looking on anxiously, the little dolphin stopped her thrashing while he carefully cut the net free.

All summer, while Molly
showed her friends Dylan
and Amina how to sail,
Dot and the other dolphins
raced and paced them, they
leapt and cavorted.

And everyone had a
whale of a summer...
until the weather turned.

21

One chilly morning, as the days got shorter, Molly was out early.

It was the first time the dolphins hadn't come to greet her.

She sailed all around, but there was no sign of them.

Further and further out to sea Molly went...

Until she noticed that the winds had changed, and it was getting harder and harder to manage the little boat.

Molly tried to turn for home but the bitter winds filled the sails, taking her further from safety, further from land.

'Help, Dad!' she cried, as the wind and the waves buffeted the little dinghy, turning her this way and that till Molly couldn't see the island any more.

She couldn't even see the lighthouse.

'Where am I?' gasped Molly.

'How will I find my way home?'

And suddenly there they were, all around her
– Dot, her young one, and the whole pod.

'My lovely dolphins!' cried Molly. 'I thought
you'd left for warmer waters!'

The dolphins swam with her, and Molly felt
so much better to have them alongside.

Fast, fast, they swam though, and she had a
job to keep pace with them.

Then off in the distance she spotted the lighthouse, flashing.

And then the harbour, her very own harbour.

'My island!' cried Molly. 'You led me back to my island!'

'And to my lovely dad!' she sighed.

As the dolphins guided her into calmer waters, Molly slowly
sailed the little *Mermaid*, side to side against the wind.

Then, 'Thank you, dolphins,' she said, quietly.
'Thank you so much for keeping me safe.'

And they peeled away, all except Dot and her calf, who
stayed alongside for a while, whirring and clicking.

Then they were gone too.

'Bye bye, my lovely dolphins,' cried Molly. 'See you next summer!'

And she watched as her beautiful friends leapt the windswept waves – all the way to the horizon and beyond.

Malachy Doyle

Malachy Doyle grew up by the sea in Northern Ireland, and after living in Wales for many years has returned to Ireland. He and his wife Liz bought an old farmhouse on a small island off the coast of Donegal, where they live with their dogs and ducks.

Malachy has had over a hundred and twenty books published, from pop-up books for toddlers to gritty teenage novels. Over the years he has won many prestigious book awards, and his work is available in around thirty languages.

As well as the five previous stories in the Molly series, *Molly and the Stormy Sea*, *Molly and the Whale*, *Molly and the Lighthouse*, *Molly and the Lockdown* and *Molly and the Shipwreck*, his recent books include *The Miracle of Hanukkah*, *Rama and Sita*, *Jack and the Jungle*, *Big Bad Biteasaurus*, *A Hundred and One Daffodils*, *The Hound of Ulster* (Bloomsbury), *Fug and the Thumps* (Firefly Press), *Cinderfella* (Walker Books) and *Ootch Cootch* (Graffeg), which is illustrated by his daughter, Hannah Doyle.

Andrew Whitson

Andrew Whitson is an award-winning artist and Belfast native who likes to be called Mr Ando! He lives in an old house which is nestled discreetly on the side of a misty hill at the edge of a magic wood, below an enchanted castle in the shadow of a giant's nose. His house looks down over Belfast Harbour, where the *Titanic* was built, and up at the Belfast Cavehill, where an American B-17 Flying Fortress bomber plane once crashed during World War II!

Mr Ando makes pictures for books in the tower of a very old church and works so late that he often gets locked in. He has therefore forged a secret magic key which he keeps at his side at all times and uses to escape from the church when there is no one else around.

Mr Ando has illustrated over twenty books under his own name, the most recent of which being the Molly series with Malachy Doyle and the award-winning Rita series of picture books with Máire Zepf.

To Bryn, *rhyf pedwar*, who loves my island too. MD

For Mal. AW

Molly and the Dolphins published by Graffeg in 2022.
Copyright © Graffeg Limited 2022.

ISBN 9781802580792

Text © Malachy Doyle, illustrations © Andrew Whitson, design and production Graffeg Limited. This publication and content is protected by copyright © 2022.

Malachy Doyle and Andrew Whitson are hereby identified as the authors of this work in accordance with section 77 of the Copyright, Designs and Patents Act 1988.

A CIP Catalogue record for this book is available from the British Library.

Mali a'r Dolffiniaid (Welsh edition)
ISBN 9781802581324

Muireann agus na Deilfeanna (Irish edition)
ISBN 9781912929276

Teaching Resources
www.graffeg.com/pages/teachers-resources

1 2 3 4 5 6 7 8 9

FSC
www.fsc.org
MIX
Paper from responsible sources
FSC® C014138